STAGE
FRIGHT!

STAGE FRIGHT!

Edgar J. Hyde

CCP

© 1999 Children's Choice Publications Ltd

Text supplied by Joan Love

ISBN 1 90201 200 3

Printed and bound in Scotland

Contents

Contents

Chapter One

The witch's gnarled and twisted hands grasped the stick firmly and stirred the contents of the cauldron. She was the eldest and also the most ugly of the three. Her huge hooked nose stopped just short of touching her top lip and when she spoke you could see that the few remaining teeth she had were blackened and broken with age. She had lost an eye some considerable years before in a battle with a white witch but, rather than wear an eye patch, she simply left the empty socket exposed, black and gruesome to the human eye.

She began to mumble as she continued stirring.

"The freshly cut tail of a gerbil, the liver of a brand new puppy, the heart of a new born lamb." She cackled and looked at her two sisters. "So far, so good," her mouth twisted into what was more an ugly grimace than a smile."Fetch me the spell book, one of you. Quickly, so that I can check what other ingredients we need."

The witch nearest made to move off, her huge black dress rustling as she did so. Like the others, she was dressed entirely in black from the top of her pointed hat to the tip of her over-large feet which were clad in huge, black buckled shoes. As with most witches, she had an abundance of warts scattered over her face, the largest of which hung from the tip of her nose. Unlike her other sisters, though, her eyes were not small and beady. They were a piercing silver which glinted dangerously as she looked about her for the mislaid spell book.

"Over there," said the third sister, pointing as she spoke. But it was not a finger which pointed, for this sister too had fought a hard battle with the same white witch years ago and lost, forfeiting her right hand and part of her arm in the process. Her hand and arm were now made of strong metal and, though at first the witch had felt rather disadvantaged, she was now able to accomplish most tasks better than ever before.

She had been able to slit the young pup's tummy, for example, without even having to use a knife, and acquiring the gerbil's tail had been really easy, and actually quite enjoyable.

She watched as her sister's eyes shone silver in the darkness as she bent to lift the spell book and bring it back to the fire over which the cauldron bubbled.

Just then, there was a huge clap of thunder as the sky grew even darker than before. Lightning forked across the sky and the three witches cackled together at the thought of the impending storm.

"A perfect night, sisters," said the first, her stagnant breath mixing with the night air as she spoke. She stopped turning the pages when she reached the spell they were looking for. She ran her blackened fingernail down the page till she got to the next ingredient she must put into the cauldron.

"Aha," she grinned maliciously. "This is one I'm going to enjoy. A young boy's freshly severed finger." She looked at her two sisters and they grinned back. "Bring him to me," she growled.

The two sisters looked delightedly at one another and left the orange glow of the flames, heading towards the bushes which encircled the clearing where they had built their fire. The boy whimpered as they approached. His wrists were raw and bleeding from his struggle to free himself from the thick ropes the witches had used to bind his arms and legs together. His blond hair hung limply on his forehead, and tear stains marked his face. He had tried to be brave, after all, 10-year-old boys don't cry, but he simply couldn't help it. He was really afraid.

The one with the silver eyes was staring at him, her eyes seeming to burn right through him, as though seeing into his very soul. The other one bent and released his feet from the ropes which tied them with one quick snip from her metal hand.

He shivered involuntarily.

"Stand up, boy," she ordered, dragging him towards her as she spoke. The boy winced, partly from the pain of her grasp, and also at the sharpness of the odour emanating from both witches.

"If I live to be a hundred," he thought to himself, "I shall never forget that smell . . . that is if I *live* at all," he thought as one of the witches pushed him in the small of the back.

He was made to walk towards the cauldron, while all the time the thunder clapped and bolts of lightening shot across the sky. As he drew nearer to the fire he could see that the eldest witch was bending down to unwrap something. She unravelled a large piece of black cloth, uncovering a vast selection of shiny steel knives. The boy drew in his breath sharply. He started to shake almost un-controllably.

The witch seemed unable to make up her mind which knife which would be best to use and was debating intently over two in particular.

When he was close enough, his two captors pushed him to his knees and began to untie his hands. The witch still looked at the knives.

"If I may make a suggestion, sister," began one, "If you're having difficulty choosing, I could sever the finger now," and she clicked her metal fingers in the air.

The boy began to cry openly.

"Shut up, snivelling little coward," said the witch, deciding eventually on a knife and lifting it into the air with a flourish. She had placed a large rock on the ground and now indicated to her sisters that they should position the boy's hand on top.

He was sobbing now, and pleading with them. "Please," he begged. "Please let me go, please don't hurt me."

Annoyed at the boy's struggles and pleas, the witch lifted the knife high into the air.

"Ready?" she asked her two sisters, who restrained the boy on either side.

They both nodded. As the knife drew nearer his hand, the child screamed and tried in vain to pull away. The cold steel glinted as it made contact and his finger, cleanly and neatly severed from his hand, fell noiselessly onto the grass. Blood spurted from the gaping wound and the witches left the boy to fall down in agony as they watched their sister excitedly lift the severed finger and throw it into the cauldron. Another bolt of thunder followed and they clapped their hands in glee and danced hysterically around the fire.

Two young girls dressed in matching leotards and tap dance shoes walked in front of the steaming cauldron and held up a large sign. Just before the curtain fell, the audience were able to read the sign "END OF ACT ONE."

Chapter Two

Their black costumes, hats and shoes discarded now in favour of their school uniforms, the three girls sat together in the school cafeteria discussing the rehearsal.

"Don't know if these plastic warts were a good idea," moaned Melissa as she looked in her mirror. "This one on my chin's stuck fast. Where on earth did you get them from?" she asked Jo.

"From the joke shop in the town," replied her friend. "The same place I got the severed finger – wasn't it great?"

"Not as great as these doughnuts," said Danny Cottrill as he passed the girls' table, swiping one of their doughnuts as he did so.

"Hey!" cried Jenny, jumping to her feet. "Give me that back."

Danny stopped and turned to face the girls. "Why, what if I don't?" he smirked. "Will you cast a spell on me?"

And he stuffed half of the stolen doughnut into his mouth.

"Yeah," shouted Jenny. "You watch yourself, Danny Cottrill, or I'll get my spell book and turn you into a fat ugly toad. Whoops," she giggled, "I almost forgot – you are a fat ugly toad." And she sat back down beside her two friends.

Danny had been too busy laughing at his own joke to overhear the last part of what Jenny had to say and made his way through the busy cafeteria, slapping people (who didn't want to be slapped) hard on the back of the head, tripping up smaller and much weaker kids who were carrying trays of food and stealing anything which was within his grasp.

"Bully," mumbled Melissa, returning her gaze to the mirror and making renewed efforts to remove the offending wart.

"Oh, I wish this thing would come off," she groaned in exasperation, just as the piece of plastic loosened its grip from her chin and fell onto the table in front of her.

"No sooner said than done," smiled Jo. "And I didn't even see you weave a spell!"

Melissa smiled back at her friend. "Didn't you hear me utter the magic words Hocus Pocus – you can wish for anything your heart desires you know – spot free skin, a place in the hockey team, a date with Jonathan . . ."

The three girls sighed as one.

"If only," Melissa breathed. "The day one of us manages to wangle a date with Jonathan will be nothing short of miraculous."

Jo rubbed at her fingernails. The black nail varnish she had just removed had left little flecks on her cuticles.

"Great rehearsal though, girls, don't you think? I'm so glad Miss Dobson found the play, it's so dramatic – you could almost hear the first formers hold their breaths this morning when we rehearsed Act 1."

Jenny agreed. "Yeah, but I have to admit it's quite a relief taking the fake arm off after rehearsal. It's quite difficult to manoeuvre the fingers."

"We could change it, I suppose," said Melissa. "I mean, it's not as though a mechanical arm featured in the original play, just that Miss Dobson thought it made *Oh Spirits Obey Us* a bit more up to date."

"No, she's right," said Jenny, flexing her hand and fingers. "We should leave it in. It does make the play a little more modern. But wasn't Jonathan brilliant this morning," she sighed longingly. "Those screams were really blood curdling, I almost believed him myself," she finished. "Anyway – where did you say Miss Dobson got this script from?" she turned to Melissa.

"Apparently," said her friend, "she was cleaning out an old cupboard in the drama room a few weeks ago when she came across it. She read it over and liked it instantly, and when she looked in old school records she realised that, although it was actually written by a former pupil about 60 years ago, it had never been performed in the school. According to what she was told, all previous attempts to stage the play had ended in failure since the pupils playing the parts of the witches' enemies had been struck down by mysterious illnesses. Weird, don't you think?"

"Definitely, and just a teensy bit scary," agreed Jo.

"Oh, don't be silly," said Jenny. "You're getting carried away with all this talk of puppies' livers and lambs' hearts. It's just a story."

Just then, the bell started to ring, signalling the end of the lunch break. Jenny scrambled about on the floor, grabbing books which had fallen out and stuffing them back into her bag.

"Must go," she called over her shoulder, after quickly finishing her juice. "A double period in history, I'm afraid – see you at 4 o'clock."

Jo and Melissa waved goodbye to their friend and made their way to the opposite end of the school.

"Double maths – ugh!" groaned Melissa, as the two entered the classroom.

"Yeah," whispered Jo, "but at least the scenery's good," and both girls laid their chins on their hands and prepared to gaze dreamily at Jonathan for the rest of the class.

Chapter Three

Next morning saw the three friends back in drama, though this time they were not on stage, but going through some of the scene changes with Miss Dobson.

"I hate these bits," muttered Melissa under her breath. "They're just so boring."

"What was that, Melissa?" asked her teacher. "Please, share whatever little gem you just imparted with the rest of the class."

Melissa cleared her throat and stood up.

"I'm sorry, Miss, I was just saying to Jenny what a good idea it had been to have a dress rehearsal yesterday."

Miss Dobson raised an eyebrow, disbelieving every word the girl said.

"Okay, Melissa, sit down and let's get on with this. We only have a couple of weeks left you know. First night will be upon us before we know it."

Eventually, after much discussion about lighting changes, who should exit when and so on and so forth, Miss Dobson called the three girls to the front of the stage.

"Okay, girls, we're going to rehearse the scene in the mortuary where the witches bring a dead body back to life. Now, remember, give it your best efforts, I want gruesome, I want evil – go on, terrify me."

Miss Dobson took her place with the rest of the class as the three witches took up the story. She had to admit, as they quickly got into character, that they were very good. They were incredibly realistic, and she actually wondered at one point if the play was going to be a bit too scary for some of the younger children in the school. She shook her head dismissively.

"No," she concluded. "Kids these days grow up so quickly it would take a lot more than a play about witches to scare them." Everything would be just fine.

On stage, the three girls had linked hands and, eyes tightly closed, they walked around the mortuary slab (or desk, for now, which would be suitably adapted on the night), slowly encircling the stiff cold body which lay there motionless, draped in a white sheet. They mumbled incantations as they walked, and Miss Dobson made a mental note to tell them to speak up a little as she was unsure which particular chant they were repeating.

She glanced sideways towards the drama room window and wondered at how dark the sky had suddenly become.

"We must be heading for a real thunder storm," she thought as she turned her attention back to the stage.

They really were very good, she thought again, as she watched the girls in action. The atmosphere was quite electric and you could have heard the proverbial pin drop in the room.

The witches had stopped encircling the body and now took up their places, one at either end of the body and one in the centre. Placing their fingertips on different parts of the body, they began to hum very quietly, gradually building up the noise until the room was filled with it. Then, as one, they stopped.

"He grows warm," smiled the witch at the centre of the body. "Let us complete our task."

Keeping one hand on the corpse and pressing the palms of the others together, they started to recite the words they hadn't said together for hundreds of years.

"From cold and dark we bid you rise
More time on earth will be your prize
To spread more evil, cast black spells
Come back to us, from brink of Hell."

They chanted the spell, over and over, their words coming faster, almost tripping over one another, till it was almost impossible to make out the words clearly. And all the time, the sky grew darker and darker. Miss Dobson watched, fascinated, as the "dead body" underneath the white sheet started to rise, as though in response to the witches' incantations.

Suddenly, the window at the far end of the room broke, and shattered into a million tiny pieces.

One of the girls who watched the play and sat nearest the window jumped up in fright and started to cry. Startled, Miss Dobson got to her feet and quickly hit the light switch. The room had grown so dark you would have sworn it was closer to midnight than midday.

"Okay, everyone, calm down," she shouted, as her pupils clamoured to see what had happened to the window. "Stay back," she ordered. "I don't want any of you cutting yourselves on the glass."

As she bent down to take a closer look, she was able to see the reason for the broken window. A small crow, no more than a few weeks old, lay amongst the shattered glass. "It must have left the nest too soon and smashed right into the window," she thought, shaking her head. "Though I wouldn't have thought one little bird would have been enough to break the window. I suppose the glass must have been weakened and the slightest thing would have broken it."

She took her handkerchief from her pocket and gathered up the tiny bird. "Stand back girls, come on now, everything's all right."

Melissa, Jo and Jenny had come off stage and joined the rest of the class looking curiously at the broken window. Miss Dobson placed the small dead bird in her waste paper basket. She would ask the janitor to remove it later. She looked up at the desk on stage with the white sheet draped over it. She climbed up the few steps to the stage and stood facing her class.

"Well done, everyone, that was great. I'll see you tomorrow for an extra rehearsal."

As the bell rang, she raised her voice to try and be heard over it. "Trolls and Hobgoblins tomorrow, remember, and bring along your costumes if they're ready."

As the class noisily gathered their things together and left the room, Miss Dobson glanced again at the white sheet. She could have sworn something had moved when the girls were reciting, but that was just plain silly. She had simply become carried away with the atmosphere, the darkening sky, the threat of thunder and lightning. Anxiously she edged towards the desk. Gingerly, and more afraid than she would have cared to admit, she lifted the edge and looked underneath. She exhaled loudly, realising then that she had been holding her breath. A bunch of books and an old pair of shoes! She should have known better! She put the sheet back gently and smiled to herself, relieved.

It wasn't until she had closed the door of the drama room behind her that she realised just how loudly her heart was beating.

Chapter Four

Jenny looked in dismay at the test paper in front of her. How she hated algebra. No matter how hard she tried, she felt she would never understand it, and it would always be as unfamiliar to her as a foreign language.

"Oh I wish I could do this," she muttered, running her fingers through her hair and chewing on the end of her pencil. Reluctantly she put pencil to paper and started to work her way through the test.

Two days later, when Mr Carter handed out the test papers, he had a huge smile for Jenny.

"Well done," he congratulated her.

"You must have put in a lot of study hours to get up to this standard – I'm delighted."

Jenny looked in disbelief at her paper. 94%! She checked her name at the top of the page, thinking Mr Carter had handed her the wrong one, but no, it was hers all right. Jo looked at her questioningly and Jenny passed her the paper.

"Wow," whispered her friend, "how did you do that?" Jenny shrugged her shoulders and opened her text book ready for that day's lesson.

Who cares how she did it, she had achieved a 94% result in a subject she had never understood. Maybe it was starting to sink in, eventually.

Weeks, even months, later, when the girls looked back at the events surrounding the play, they would realise just how early their wishes had begun to come true.

Silly things like Melissa wishing her wart would come off, Jenny's algebra test, and, later, Jo wishing her mum would buy her decent trainers. No sooner had they voiced their wish, than it happened. But they didn't start to get spooked until the day they wished harm on Danny Cottrill.

The sun was shining and most of the students were outside watching the fourth formers' Sports Day. The events were taking place in different parts of the field, but the girls were watching the hurdles as Jonathan, their hero, was the favourite to win. The starting gun was fired and the boys started running. Jonathan was on the outside of the track and, on his right, ran Danny Cottrill. The boys were almost neck and neck for most of the race until Danny fell and, as he did so, he seemed to deliberately stick his foot in Jonathan's path meaning that he, too, was brought down.

"Pig!" shouted Melissa. "Why'd he have to go and do that? Jonathan was running really well. He'd have won for sure if that idiot hadn't pulled him down with him!" She sat down, disgusted.

Jenny agreed. "Sometimes I really wish he would do himself some serious harm, the bully."

The race continued, of course, and Jonathan slowly got to his feet, checking for damage as he did so. He had cut his knee, though not badly, and limped over towards Danny to offer him a helping hand. Danny wasn't moving. Jonathan leaned closer, just as the school first aider ran on to the track.

"I think he must have knocked himself out when he fell," said Jonathan. "Maybe he's got concussion."

The first aider quickly checked the boy over and decided that the best course of action was to call for an ambulance. Danny was stretchered off the playing field and, lights flashing and siren wailing, was taken to the local hospital.

Next morning, Mr Perrie, the Headmaster called an assembly where he told the school of Danny's injuries. Not only had the boy broken both legs as he fell, he had suffered some sort of internal haemorrhage and had slipped into a coma. His family were around his bedside and had been told that, although it was possible Danny would survive, they should really expect the worst.

Jenny covered her mouth with her hands.

"Oh my God," she breathed as Melissa

and Jo looked at her. "I wished that on him. Remember? In the sports field? I actually wished something serious would happen to Danny, and now it has."

"Oh don't be silly, Jenny," started Jo. "You can't wish someone into a coma!"

"Can't you?" asked Jenny. "I'm not so sure. Let's take a long hard look at what's been happening over the past few weeks."

The girls had by now left the assembly hall and had stopped outside their next class. Aided by Jenny, Melissa started recounting all the things they had wished for which had now come true. Though sceptical to begin with, there were so many things which had actually come true that Jo had to agree there was perhaps a bit more than sheer coincidence involved.

"But how . . . I mean, I don't understand why all of a sudden this should be happening to us," said Jo. "How many times have you closed your eyes and made a wish, hoping against hope it just might come true, which of course it never does, and now for some inexplicable reason we're being granted everything we ask for? Why?"

"The play," said Jenny, quietly. "I think everything is somehow linked to the play. Think about it, you two, this all started to happen when we took on the roles of the witches."

Mrs Cadzow leaned on the door jamb and looked over at the three girls.

"Is there something I should know, girls? Have you been exempted from my classroom and no-one bothered to tell me?" she asked.

"Oh, sorry, Miss, we were just coming,"

stuttered Melissa, as the three girls made their way into the classroom.

Before she took her seat, she whispered to her two friends "Remember that old saying – be very careful what you wish for, it just might come true – I think we should start to be careful about . . ."

"MELISSA!" shouted Mrs Cadzow. "Are you or are you not a member of this class? If you are, please sit down, take out your books, and pay attention to today's lesson."

The bell signalling the end of their day seemed to take an interminable time to ring. The girls gathered at the school gates, and Melissa took her copy of the play from her bag.

"Geraldine Somers," she read aloud. "She was the person who wrote the play, and I think we should start doing a bit of research on her. The more time I have to think about these wishes, the more convinced I am it has something to do with the play, and the author seems as good a person to start with as any."

Jenny and Jo nodded in agreement.

"Let's see, tomorrow's Saturday, so we can go to the Library in the morning and see if we can find any record of her, you know, where she lives now, if she's written any other plays and so on."

"But remember," said Jo, "this play was written at least 60 years ago and if Geraldine was, say, 13 or 14 when she wrote it, she'll be quite old by now. We'll have to tread very carefully if we do find her, we don't want to go upsetting an old lady needlessly."

Agreeing to meet the following morning at 9 am sharp outside the Library ("9 am on a Saturday morning," groaned Jenny, "there goes my lie-in.") the girls parted company.

Chapter Five

The girls had been searching unsuccessfully for the best part of an hour when suddenly Melissa found what she was looking for.

"There she is," she said excitedly, running her finger down the page. "Look – Geraldine Somers, born 10.07.20 – that means she must be what, 79 years old by now. So if she wrote the play when she was 14, it's actually nearer to 65 years old. Great. Now, where does she live?"

"Look, Melissa," said Jo quietly, pointing to the opposite side of the page. Under the farthest away column, an entry had been penned in showing that

Geraldine Somers had died on the 14th of April 1982. Jo sighed.

"That'll be that then – we can't talk to a ghost," she said resignedly.

The three girls stood silently staring at the information on the page. What could they do now, but forget the whole idea of research? Jenny closed the book and put it back on the shelf they had taken it from.

"Come on, you two, let's go. No point in standing here." Jenny linked arms with her two friends and the three left the Library.

Melissa stopped suddenly.

"Wait a minute," she said to her two friends. "We can visit the grave, can't we? She must be buried in the local graveyard. Her last known address in the book was in our village, so it makes sense that she must be buried here. Yes, that's it," she nodded her head excitedly, "We'll go visit her grave."

Jenny and Jo looked at one another, both feeling a lot less enthusiastic than Melissa appeared to be.

"But, Melissa, I really can't see the point of . . ." began Jo.

"The point is," interrupted Melissa, "that it's the only starting point we have. Don't you see – we have nowhere else to go. We must visit the grave, we simply must, if we want to find out anything. Jenny?" she looked enquiringly at her other friend.

"Well," began Jenny, slowly, "I suppose I would like to get to the bottom of what's been going on, but I don't know if . . ."

"That's settled then," Melissa interrupted again. "Let's go, it won't take us long to walk."

"Melissa, wait," said Jenny. "I can't go right now. I have to go shopping with my mum this afternoon and if we walk to and from the graveyard I won't be back in time to meet her. I'm either going to have to opt out or do this later."

Melissa looked at Jo.

"Sorry, Melissa, I promised to take my niece ice skating this afternoon. I could come with you when I get back, though. I should be home around tea time."

Melissa sighed heavily, disappointed that they couldn't begin straight away. She wasn't exactly renowned for her patience.

"Okay," she agreed reluctantly, "can we all meet at the gates of the graveyard at 4.30? That should give us just enough daylight hours to find the gravestone and check things out. And remember, wear something warm, it'll be really cold up there."

The local graveyard was located at the very top of a steep hill and was notoriously cold, especially on a dark November night. Jo trembled inwardly at the thought of what they were going to be doing later that evening, but said nothing, not wanting to put a damper on Melissa's plans.

As they again went their separate ways, Melissa shouted over her shoulder to one of the girls to remember to bring a torch. And a stake - just in case.

"Just in case of what?" Jo glanced worriedly at Jenny.

"Vampires," Jenny told her friend. Then, seeing the look of horror on her friend's face, she laughed. "Joke," she smiled.

"Honestly, she's joking. There's no such

thing, Jo, you've been watching too many scary movies."

Jo grinned sheepishly. "No, no, I knew all the time, I knew she was joking. Really, I did," she tried to convince her unconvinced friend.

Jenny slipped her arm through Jo's. "It's all right, Jo, I'm not too happy about going to a graveyard either, but it'll be fine, you'll see."

Chapter Six

4.30 prompt. Melissa glanced at her watch. Where were the others? Just at that she heard the chatter of her friends' voices as they reached the top of the hill and joined her.

". . . and that was when I had to have the bandage applied," finished Jo. "So embarrassing. There was Katy, skating and twirling like a professional, and I had to go and fall. And of course it just wouldn't stop bleeding, which was even worse, but when the attendant insisted I go and visit the treatment room, well I just thought I would die of shame. I mean, 14 years old and I'm going to have a lovely great scar on my knee which will be just beautiful for the Christmas Disco. Great."

"Hey, Melissa, been here long?" asked Jenny.

Melissa moved position, stamping her feet in an attempt to keep warm. "No," she half smiled, "I just arrived."

It really was bitterly cold tonight, the paths leading in different directions and glistening with frost in the semi-darkness.

"Okay," said Melissa, taking charge as always, "this is the plan. I think we'll have to split up, each of us taking a section of the graveyard until we find the grave. It's got to be the quickest way of doing it - there's just no point in us covering the same ground together. So what do you think of us going our own way just now and meeting back here at, say, 7 pm? That should give us enough time."

"But what if we find the grave before then?" asked Jenny sensibly.

"Well, the cemetery's maybe not that big," said Melissa thoughtfully. "What about if we make our way to the mausoleum for 6 pm – do you think that would be enough time?"

Jenny shivered involuntarily at the use of the word "mausoleum". The grand, imposing building which stood at the edge of the cemetery had been erected over a hundred years ago by a Mr Carruthers in memory of his wife. It stood, a proud monument to the memory of Mrs Carruthers, and now housed not only her body, but also that of Mr Carruthers himself and most of the Carruthers family. Though Jenny supposed, grudgingly, that it was a beautiful building, it gave her the creeps, and she tended to hurry past it as quickly as she could if she ever had to go that way. She glanced at the building's tall domes then looked away quickly.

What she really wanted to do right now was turn on her heels and go back home. She hated scary things and places, and hated too how she was so easily coerced into doing things she didn't want to. She sighed. She did really like Melissa and Jo, though, and didn't want to let them down.

"Sure," she said, with mock enthusiasm. "6 pm should be just fine. Who's taking which path?"

After some discussion, the girls set off, each with their own private thoughts, and each equally determined that they would be the one to find the gravestone. Jenny was more determined than the others that she would be back before darkness really started to fall. She wanted this search to be over with as quickly as possible.

The graveyard forked off into three different roads and the girls took one each. Jenny walked along slowly, scanning each stone as she walked.

"David Fisher, beloved husband and father. Born 1902, died 1964,"she read from the first.

"Suzanna Bellingham, aged 7 years. Our beautiful daughter, gone to be with the angels. Born 1935, died 1942."

Jenny stopped and stared.

"How awful," she thought. "How sad, losing your child when she was so young."

She wondered what had happened to the little girl, an accident perhaps or an illness which could probably be cured nowadays, though not back in 1942. She tore herself away and tried to concentrate.

"Come on, Jen," she chastised herself. "You're not here to ponder over people's deaths, you're here to find one particular stone."

She moved on, her eyes concentrating on the name on each gravestone. She did come across a Geraldine once, but the surname was wrong and the dates didn't tie in.

She walked past gravestones which were so old they had toppled over, and she passed others which had been newly erected and had fresh flowers strewn in front of them. She couldn't quite make up her mind which ones she hated most.

After an hour, she had covered the whole of one side of the path and turned to make her way back down the other.

It was growing darker now and she found that she was having to step closer to the graves so that she could make out the inscriptions. She was sorry she'd forgotten to bring a torch, and wondered how the other two girls were faring.

Half way back down the path, she felt the first splash of rain.

"Great," she thought to herself, "just what you want. Stuck in the middle of a graveyard on a cold November night with rain pouring down on top of you!"

She squinted up at the blackening sky. The rain grew heavier and she quickened her pace, making her way towards the mausoleum. With a bit of luck either Jo or Melissa would have found the grave by now and they could all get out of this place.

The remaining gravestones were merely given cursory glances as Jenny walked hurriedly now in the direction of the mausoleum. There was no sign of her two friends and Jenny stood outside for a few minutes, the rain much heavier now, dripping off her jacket and soaking into her denims.

"They must have gone inside," she thought to herself. "You'd have to be mad to stand out here getting wet."

She turned and walked up the few steps to the mausoleum and turned the handle. The solid door opened slowly and Jenny pushed it creakily open. She caught her breath. It was as dark inside here as it was outside in the cemetery and everything smelt damp and musty. She stepped forward. To her right she could see the tomb erected by Mr Carruthers in memory of his wife. The white marble tomb was just visible in the darkness, as were the stone pillars placed at each corner. Ornate drawings and inscriptions adorned the walls, though Jenny could not make out exactly what they were.

"Melissa? Jo?" she tried to call, though her voice was no more than a whisper. She cleared her throat and tried again, calling to her friends a bit more loudly this time. She had started to edge her way forwards now and was aware of another huge tomb on her left. This one had the body shape of a man carved in marble etched on top of it. Jenny, her eyes growing more accustomed to the darkness, could make out the outline of his face.

"How creepy," she thought, unable to understand why anyone would want a likeness of themselves put in such an awful place as this, which stank of rotting flesh and death.

She heard scuffling at her feet and jumped, her hand brushing one of the tombs as she did so. Though she couldn't be sure, she thought she saw a tail disappear through a hole in the wall.

"Oh, no, rats," she thought, her immediate instinct being to run. She steadied herself and removed her hand from the tomb. It felt wet and slimy. She lifted it closer to her face and saw that her hand was coated in slime, and parts of it appeared to be moving. Maggots! They were crawling all over the tomb, and all over her! She tried to shake the horrible creatures from her hand, and barely managed to stifle a scream as she turned to run from this horrible place. She could see that thousands of maggots were pouring from the eyes and nose of the marble figure on the tomb. She had to get out of there, and fast.

At that precise moment, the heavy wooden door banged shut behind her.

Chapter Seven

"Jenny, over here," she heard her friend's voice. "We've been waiting for you."

She looked down towards the front of the mausoleum and was able to make out the figures of Melissa and Jo.

"Thank God," she breathed, stifling a small sob as she almost ran towards her two friends. "I'm so pleased to see you," she said. "I just had the most awful experience. I really, really think we should get out of here, now."

Melissa and Jo half turned towards her. "Don't be silly," said Melissa. "Everything's all right now. Come on, come and sit beside me."

The two girls were sitting on a low bench in front of a raised up platform, almost like an altar. As Melissa turned fully towards her friend, she stretched out both arms to her. Except that something was missing.

"Your hand!" gasped Jenny, stepping back in horror. "What's happened to your hand?"

For Melissa's hand was no longer there, instead her arm seemed to stop just inside the sleeve of her jacket.

"I don't understand," gasped Jenny. "Are you playing tricks on me," she half sobbed. "Because if you are, they're definitely not amusing."

She turned to her other friend.

"Jo, Jo, talk to me."

"Calm down," began Jo. "There's no need to get hysterical."

And as she turned to look her friend full in the face, Jenny gasped in horror and screamed. Jo's right eye was missing.

"Don't scream, you silly girl. It's only an eye socket. Gosh, I didn't know you could be such a baby."

Jenny covered her face with both her hands. She must be having a bad dream, surely. There was no other explanation for this. She opened her eyes and looked again at her two friends. To her horror, Melissa and Jo were now undergoing some sort of bizarre transformation before her very eyes. Their skin had turned brown and cracked before it started to fall in small pieces from their faces. Underneath were much older faces which Jenny recognised as belonging to the witches from the play. Their faces were covered in warts, lined and wrinkled, with huge, hooked noses and blackened stumpy teeth. Their clothes too fell away and were replaced by the black cloaks Jenny had by now become familiar with. A foul odour permeated the mausoleum and Jenny's terror was complete.

She wanted to run but knew she had to pass the tombs containing the rotting, dead bodies and the floor which seemed to be alive with squirming maggots. She felt herself being prodded from behind and turned around to see who was there. She drew in her breath sharply. The third witch. The one whose part she took in the play.

"What are you doing – what do you want from me?" she asked falteringly.

"We don't want anything from you, my dear," replied one. "It's what you want from us," that matters, don't you see?"

"No, no, I'm afraid I don't." Jenny tried to stop her voice from wavering.

The three witches now encircled her, their fetid breaths touching her face as they walked slowly around, their dusty black cloaks billowing around their feet.

"So stupid, so unutterably stupid," cackled the witch who was missing an eye. "The play, my pretty one, the play. *Oh Spirits Obey Us*, remember? The one you're performing at school? Don't you know what it's about? Don't you know how dangerous it is to dabble in witch-craft when you know nothing about it?"

"But, but, it's only a play," stammered Jenny, desperately trying to keep calm.

The witches stopped moving.

"Only a play, is it?" said the first witch, in a menacingly low voice. "You stupid girl, don't you know anything? You can't just recite spells, dabble in witchcraft, chop off fingers, then just walk away from it. Witchcraft's a very dangerous thing, you know."

She pushed her face closer to Jenny's and the young girl recoiled as far as she dared, only to be pushed forward again by the bony fingers of the witch behind her.

"We didn't really chop the finger off," she stuttered. "Only pretended to."

"Shut up," the witch snarled. "I'm the one who's speaking." She ran her bony fingers through Jenny's hair, causing the girl to shiver, but she stood her ground nonetheless.

"Aha, she has guts, has she?" cackled the witch as the girl stood firm. "Why do you think we waited for you this evening? We wanted to offer you something, my pretty."

She looked at her two colleagues and both nodded and smirked in the girl's direction. Using the one hand she did possess, she took hold of Jenny's. Her fingers were long and bony and unbelievably cold. Jenny desperately wanted to pull away.

"How would you like to join us," she asked the girl. "Become a witch, a real witch, I mean, not someone playing a part in a play. Someone who can do this."

And she spat at the girl's feet. Jenny looked down and saw the witch's spittle spread and grow bigger on the floor of the mausoleum before it gradually began to take shape. First the tail developed, followed by the long, sharp teeth and furry body, until gradually the spit had turned into a large brown rat! The biggest rat, in fact, that Jenny had ever seen. She moved her feet backwards, but noted that the rat did not move away, seeming content to stare at her from its position on the floor.

The witch smiled, a broad, almost toothless smile, and her two sisters cackled with laughter. The one with the missing eye clapped her hands.

"Well done, sister, I'd forgotten that old trick." And she too spat on the floor, her spittle also spreading and becoming larger before transforming into another rat, this one even bigger than before if that were possible. Not to be outdone, the third sister repeated the process, and soon there were dozens of rats, some brown, some black, but none of them moving and all of them seeming to stare right at Jenny.

"Please, let me wake up," the young girl prayed. "Let me open my eyes and this nightmare will be over."

She closed her eyes and blinked hard but when she opened them again the scene in front of her was exactly as it had been before.

"We're still here, my dear," cackled the first witch, almost as though she were able to read the young girl's mind. "And we're still looking for recruits. Come on, my pretty," she rubbed her bony finger along the girl's chin. "You'd have such fun, you know. Let's see, now, who else do you dislike? Apart from young Danny Cottrill?" The witch smiled. "We sorted him for you now, didn't we? He's still on a life support machine, but you could be the one to perform the magic Jenny. You. You could cast the evil spells. You need never be afraid of anyone again. No-one would ever be able to hurt you, and we could give you that power. Come on now, what do you say?"

Jenny was horrified.

"Danny? You did that to Danny? How could you, how awful . . ."

The witch interrupted. "No, my dear, you did it. You wished harm on the boy, did you not? And since we have to obey you, in accordance with the title of the play, we were only carrying out your wishes."

"But everyone says things they don't mean sometimes," said Jenny. "I didn't really want anything bad to happen to Danny." She moved her foot slightly, looking down as she did so. The rats still stared up at her but none of them moved.

"Then you'll have to be more careful about what you wish for, won't you. But I'm not at all convinced that I believe you.

I think you'd make a great witch, and we're so in need of some young blood."

She moved towards the girl, kicking out at one of the rats as she did so. The rat reacted for the first time, angrily biting at Jenny's ankle as though she were to blame. The girl cried out and bent to rub at her ankle.

"Please let me go," she pleaded with the witches. "Please, my parents will be wondering where I've got to. I have to go home, please."

"Don't be stupid, we can't let you go now. You're going to be one of us. Be patient, dear, we just have to recite a little spell, it won't take long. Come, sisters, join hands and you, my dear, you must concentrate on what we are saying, for you will have to join with us at the end, and take a vow to be a follower of Satan and all things evil."

The witches started their chant, walking slowly around the girl, the rats now scuttled in all directions in order to escape the sharp kick of the witches' feet. Jenny was trembling from head to toe and trying desperately to think of a way out. If she could just break though the circle of the witches' hands and run towards the entrance to the mausoleum she would perhaps be able to avoid the rats, although she would be certain to encounter the millions of slimy maggots which crawled all over the tombs and the floor. She swallowed hard. She could stand the maggots, she decided. She had to get out of here.

As she looked up towards the back of the mausoleum she saw to her horror that one of the tombs was opening. A skeletal hand was pushing back the marble lid and

Chapter Seven

she could just see the skull-like head beginning to appear.

Jenny fainted.

Chapter Eight

Meanwhile, outside in the cemetery, Melissa and Jo, the real Melissa and Jo, had found the grave of Geraldine Somers. They had bumped into one another just outside the mausoleum, both having exhausted the graves in the parts of the cemetery they had explored, when by chance they spotted a few graves tucked away in the corner just beside the entrance. And sure enough, there it was, clearly engraved with the author's name. Both girls bent down, wiping the by now heavy rain out of their eyes.

"Geraldine Somers – so we found you at last," breathed Melissa.

She brushed her fingers over the lettering on the grave, taking in the woman's date of birth, when she died, and all the time thinking how plain and unobtrusive the lettering was in comparison to some of the stones she had looked at earlier. There was a vase of fairly fresh flowers placed at the foot of the grave, and Melissa wondered idly who had placed them there.

"So you found me, girls," came the sound of a soft, whispery voice.

Jo and Melissa looked quizzically at one another.

"Who said that? Jenny?" The girls looked around.

The howling of the wind and the steady beat of the rain as it splashed heavily onto the ground sounded in the girls' ears. Melissa pushed her hair back from her face and smiled at Jo.

"We're hearing things – the wind's playing tricks on us, that's all."

But again the voice came, still soft but this time a little more clearer.

"I've been waiting for you, girls, I'm so glad you're here at last."

The two girls stood up swiftly, almost falling backwards in their haste, grabbing on to one another as they did so.

"Where is it coming from?" asked Jo. "I can hear a voice, but I can't see any-one."

She held on to Melissa fearfully.

"Please don't be afraid girls, please," the voice was stronger and more insist-ent now. "I really have to talk with you. Please, bend closer to the stone again, I need you both to listen to me very care-fully."

Melissa and Jo looked at each other in bewilderment but, mainly because they didn't know what else to do, they did as they were bid and walked forward to kneel in front of Geraldine Somers' gravestone. As they knelt on the wet grass, there was an audible sigh of relief.

"Thank you, girls, I hoped you'd be the ones to help, so please listen very carefully to what I have to say. I am the spirit of Geraldine Somers. I no longer have the power to materialise – my spirit has been growing steadily weaker over the years and I am afraid that you will be unable to see me. You can, however, hear my voice and hopefully, once I have related my story to you, you will be able to help."

The rain was beating down onto the girls' bent forms and the sky was almost completely black. Melissa and Jo were afraid – they no longer wanted to be here, in the graveyard, they wanted to forget the whole idea of finding the author's grave – they wanted to forget the entire play for that matter. But before either of the girls could move, the voice spoke again.

"The play, *Oh Spirits Obey Us*, you must know that I was the person responsible for writing it, God help me. I know that you two and your friend are playing the parts of the three witches in it, and that is why I must speak to you. You see, although the play was written over 60 years ago, it has never been performed on stage. There is always a series of accidents which befalls anyone who tries to help me stop the evil witches carrying out their plan. Anyone who has played the parts of the witches up until now has been very happy to have all their wishes come true, and been totally disinterested in helping me to break the witches' evil hold. So when I knew you girls weren't happy with recent events, well, it was like a breath of fresh air." The voice paused briefly. "It's all my fault," she began again. "I wrote the words to the play and, unwittingly or not, I conjured up those evil sisters and I will have to be the one to cast them back into the darkness where they belong. Of course, I can't do it myself and so I have to put myself at your mercy and ask, no, plead, for you girls to help."

"But, what can we do?" asked Melissa. "The witches, or spirits, can't be real, surely?"

She looked at Jo. Jo didn't reply but the look on her face said more than words ever could.

"Yeah, I know," nodded Melissa wryly. "I'm talking to a gravestone – how real can things get?"

The voice started again. "We don't have a lot of time, girls, so please hear what I have to say. In the past, the girls playing the parts of the witches have seemed to actually take on their characters as well as the parts they are playing. Decent, well mannered children have turned into nasty, evil people who become accustomed to having their wishes come true. In the course of the rehearsals, anyone who is seen to oppose these girls meets with a nasty accident – look back at the school records – you'll see that I'm speaking the truth. If, however, the play ever does have an opening night, it must not be performed the way it is written. If it is, everyone who is in the audience will become spellbound. What we must try to do, without anyone else's knowledge, is change some parts of the play, break the spell and consign these evil witches to hell. By doing so you will also manage to free my trapped spirit. I can have no rest while the witches are allowed to carry on their evil work."

She paused. Melissa wiped some rain from her face and sat back on her heels.

"I know this is such a huge amount of information for you young girls to take in. And I know how unbelievable this whole story must seem to you, but I'm begging you both. Will you help?"

Before the girls could reply, they heard a loud scream coming from the direction of the mausoleum. Almost as one, they jumped quickly to their feet.

"Jenny!"

Chapter Nine

They both ran in the direction of the huge building and quickly climbed the stairs. As they pushed open the door, they were horrified by what they saw. Their eyes already accustomed to the darkness, they could quite clearly see their friend at the far end of the mausoleum. And she was not alone. As Geraldine Somers had said, the three witches were indeed walking the earth, practising their evil magic. In fact they were right here, practising on their poor friend! Melissa grabbed hold of Jo's hand.

"Come on, quickly, we have to help her." Jo held back.

"Melissa, look." Melissa followed her friend's gaze to the moving carpet of maggots which lay before her. She gasped and put her hand to her mouth.

"Not maggots, please not maggots," she thought. She hated maggots. They were everywhere, crawling over the tombs and even making their way up the pillars. Swallowing hard, Melissa took hold of Jo's hand.

"We have to do this," she said. "Come on, Jo, we have to go help Jenny."

She would never forget the crunching noise under her feet as she and her friend went bravely forward into the heart of the mausoleum.

The witches were walking around Jenny in a circle now, and the two girls tried to conceal themselves behind one of the many pillars before deciding on the best way to help their friend.

When Melissa heard the scuttling noise at her feet, she didn't even have to look down, she knew it would be rats. Jo stifled a scream and clung tightly to her friend.

The witches' chant was growing louder and the girls knew they would have to make a move soon if they were to help Jenny. At almost the same time as Jenny saw the tomb open, so too did Melissa and Jo. But where Jenny mercifully fainted, there was no such release for the other two girls. They clung to each other in terror as the glowing red eyes of the skull emerged from the tomb.

"What's going on in there?" shouted a voice from the back of the mausoleum. As the girls looked up, both doors were thrown open and two burly policemen brandishing torches came inside. In an instant, the tomb lid slid back into place, the maggots disappeared, as did the rats, and the witches simply seemed to vanish into thin air. Melissa and Jo ran from their hiding place to the front of the mausoleum and knelt beside their friend. Jo shook her shoulder.

"Jenny, Jenny, can you hear me? It's Jo. Jo and Melissa. Are you all right?"

Jenny's eyes opened ever so slowly. "Have they gone?" she asked, her voice no more than a whisper.

"They've gone, Jenny," Jo reassured her. "Everything's going to be all right. Can you sit up?"

Helped by Melissa and Jo, Jenny managed to pull herself into an upright position. A brief flicker of fear crossed her face.

"Are you really Jo and Melissa? You're

not going to change into those awful spirits again, are you?"

Melissa held out both arms to hug her friend.

"It's really us, Jen," she said.

Jenny leaned forward into her friend's embrace.

"You've got both hands, Melissa," she smiled. "It really is you."

Just before she fainted for the second time that night, the two police officers heard her say: "And you have your eye back, Jo, I'm so glad you have your eye back."

"Concussion," one of the officers mouthed to the other. "Let's get her out of here."

Chapter Ten

"You're very lucky, young lady," said the nurse at the hospital as she tucked Jenny's jeans back into her boots.

"I don't know whether it was a rat or not, but whatever nipped your ankle was prevented from breaking the skin by your boots."

"I, I'm not sure either," said Jenny, for the busy Casualty Department was so far removed from the horrors of the mausoleum that she had begun to wonder if she hadn't imagined the whole thing. But then the nurse did say there was a mark on her ankle as though something had tried to bite her . . .

The nurse drew back the screen and Melissa and Jo were allowed to see their friend.

"Your mother should be here soon," said the nurse as she left to attend to the next patient. Then, putting her head back round the screen, "and don't sit on the bed," she admonished the two girls.

Melissa and Jo got up from where they had positioned themselves on either side of their friend.

"Oops – all we seem to have done tonight is gotten ourselves into trouble," smiled Melissa.

"Yeah," agreed Jo. "Though I think I'd far rather get into trouble from a nurse than three evil witches in a spooky graveyard."

"So, what now?" asked Jenny.

"Well, what you don't know is that,

while you were alone in the mausoleum, Jo and I found the grave of Geraldine Somers and managed to speak with her," said Melissa.

"Speak with her? How can you speak with a ghost?" questioned Jenny, wondering if, indeed, she was suffering from concussion.

Jo and Melissa exchanged amused glances.

"Yeah, we know it sounds bizarre," said Jo, "but it actually did happen."

And between them the two girls recounted word for word what Geraldine Somers had had to say to them from her grave.

When they had finished Jenny nodded her head slowly.

"It all makes sense, then, and I didn't dream any of it, did I? The witches, the play, the missing hand and eye, the whole thing actually did happen. Gosh – just what have we got mixed up in?"

"What, indeed," said Melissa. "The question we have to ask ourselves now is, do we walk away from Geraldine and all the problems surrounding the play, or do we help her?"

"And everyone else," rejoined Jo. "Remember what she said – if the play takes place on opening night and is performed word for word from the written transcript, everyone in the audience will be spellbound." She shook her head and looked down at the floor. "If you ask me," she said to her two friends "we don't have any choice."

"But there are only a few days to go till opening night," said Jenny, "and a full dress rehearsal on Thursday. We don't have long to decide how we're going to sabotage the play."

Melissa looked thoughtful.

"Geraldine said we couldn't follow the play word for word. So what if we change the words around? What if we don't recite the spells exactly as they're written, don't recite the chants as we should? That would work, wouldn't it?" she looked questioningly at her friends.

Jenny agreed. "Yes, that sounds hopeful, Melissa, but as soon as we get the words wrong someone else on stage, or Miss Dobson for that matter, will stop the play and correct us. How do we get round that problem?"

Melissa thought some more. "We miss rehearsals," she said slowly. "Don't you see – Miss Dobson would correct us in rehearsals, but there's no way she would stop and correct the real thing on the opening night. Not with the assembly hall full of parents and other teachers. Far too embarrassing to admit that your three leading ladies have got it wrong!"

"And just how do we excuse ourselves from rehearsals?" asked Jo.

"Well, Jenny's got the perfect excuse, hasn't she? Banged her head, hurt her ankle, needs a few days' rest. No problem. And you and I? Hmm, let's see, a bad head cold? A sore throat? Any sort of minor ailment would do," said Melissa. "Take your pick."

"And then we all make remarkable recoveries on opening night," said Jo, "by which time we've re-written the parts of the play we need to and learnt all the new words!"

"Simplicity itself," smiled Melissa.

"Leave the re-writes to me and I'll bribe my brother to bring them over to your houses – if we're pretending to have colds and sore throats I know for sure my parents won't be happy for me to leave the house. I knew my brother would have his uses some day."

"The cemetery?" they heard the voice from the other end of the corridor.

"Oh no, my mother," groaned Jenny, instantly feeling even more unwell than she had before.

"Inside the mausoleum? What on earth was she doing in there? Where is she? Let me see her, please? Jenny? Jenny? Where are you?"

Her mother's high pitched voice carried right the way down the hospital corridor until her head poked around the screened-off bed and she found her daughter. She threw her arms around the girl and hugged her so tightly she could hardly breathe.

"We'll be off, then," said Jo as she and Melissa made to leave. Jenny tried to wave to her friends but her mother gripped her so tightly she was unable to move her arms.

"Mum, I'm fine," she struggled to get the words out. "Really, I just had a bit of a fall – there's nothing broken."

"Fine? Fine?" screeched her mother. "Have you any idea the things that have been running through my mind ever since the police knocked on my door this evening? And then to be told they found you in the mausoleum? Are you mad? What were you doing in there? You, Jenny, of all people, my Jenny who's scared of her own shadow?"

"It's a long story, Mum, but right now I feel a bit tired. Can I tell you later?"

"Tired?" questioned her mother. "But you mustn't sleep just now dear, you may have some sort of concussion. Did you hit your head when you fell? Wait there, do you hear, don't move. I'm going to fetch a doctor to see exactly what sort of condition you're in. Maybe you shouldn't come home with me tonight – maybe it'd be an idea to spend a night here under observation."

As her mother left the cubicle, Jenny put her head back on her pillow and closed her eyes. Her mother did go on, but after her ordeal earlier that night, she actually found the high pitched screech strangely reassuring. Maybe it was concussion, after all . . .

Chapter Eleven

"Jo, where are you?" shouted Jo's dad from the hall downstairs.

"In the loo," the girl croaked. "What's wrong?"

"Melissa's younger brother's just delivered a package for you – I'm off out to work now, but I'll leave it on the telephone table for you and you can come down and get it. I'd bring it up, but I'm running late as it is."

Jo appeared at the top of the stairway. "It's all right, Dad. I'll come down in a minute. Melissa said she'd send over some magazines for me, it's nothing important."

"Okay, must go, see you later sweet-heart," Dad called as he wrestled with the door chain.

"Maybe if you put your briefcase down first?" suggested his daughter.

Putting down his briefcase with one hand and putting the half-eaten toast from the other hand into his mouth, her dad was able to release the security chain and open the front door.

"Bye," he called again as he pulled the door shut behind him.

Jo shook her head. "Fathers," she thought. "Worse than kids sometimes."

She bounded down the stairs and grabbed the brown envelope from its place on the table. It had been two days now since the graveyard incident, and there was only one more day to go before the opening night of the play. Going into the kitchen, Jo made herself some fresh tea and toast, set everything on a tray and took them back upstairs to her bedroom. She opened her curtains a little to allow some grey November light into the room and settled down to look for Melissa's corrections.

Almost the same scene was taking place in Jenny's house, as she scanned through the pages to see the changes Melissa had made. Her friend had used a yellow highlighter pen so that the alterations were easy to spot, and Jenny set about re-learning her lines. Whatever she did, she mustn't say the correct words on the night. She must concentrate and learn the spells the way Melissa had written them.

Meanwhile, in school, Miss Dobson was tearing her hair out.

"No, no, no," she admonished. "That's not when you're supposed to exit – you have to wait until the trolls enter, then you can leave."

She pushed her fingers through her already unruly hair and took a deep breath. She should have listened to the Headmaster – he had told her about the play's history, and she had been stubborn enough to persist that she would be able to successfully stage a performance. Now look what had happened – her three leading girls were ill! All three of them! And on top of that no-one on stage seemed to have any idea where they were supposed to stand, never mind what they were supposed to say. She wondered if they were aware what production they were starring in!

"Look, everyone, I know this is difficult," she began in the loudest voice she could muster. "And especially when we're missing our three witches, though their respective parents assure me they will be here on opening night. So for now, if we can just pretend they are here, use our imagination a little, and concentrate on the parts we're meant to be playing, perhaps we can get through this without me murdering one of you."

Some of the pupils giggled, forcing Miss Dobson to smile.

"And perhaps we can actually make it to opening night, and put on a perform-ance both the school and your parents will be proud of?"

Lots of throat clearing and head nod-ding from the stage.

"Okay, from the beginning of that scene, Grant, please? And remember,

Hobgoblins do not chew bubble gum."

Chapter Twelve

The bouquet of flowers lay in the small wash-hand basin in the Headmaster's office. He would present them to Miss Dobson after the play tonight. He checked in the mirror to see that his tie was straight and wiped a chocolate crumb from the side of his mouth. That was the trouble with these school performances, he found it so hard to resist the donations of home baking the mothers handed in to the school. Particularly Mrs Castle's home baked chocolate chip cookies. He moved the notch of his belt so it would sit easier on his ever-expanding waistline and left his office to make his way to the assembly hall.

There was an air of excitement as people entered the hall. Everyone attending would have someone close to them who would be performing on the stage that night, whether it be family or perhaps just the child of a friendly neighbour. Younger brothers and sisters squirmed in their seats, most of them being kept quiet with a bar of chocolate in one hand and a fizzy drink in the other, with the promise of ice cream at the interval.

The stage set itself had been designed by the fourth formers, helped by Miss Dobson. Black, obviously, provided the main colour, and bats, spiders and creepy crawlies in every shape and form were suspended from the ceiling.

Some of the school children had made programmes which they sold to any willing audience members as they entered the hall. Unfortunately they had used black and orange ink cartridges which were unsuitable for the ancient school laser printer, so the ink remained wet, and most of the audience took their seats sporting orange and black faces where their inky hands had touched.

The hall was filling up rapidly. Melissa had looked out from behind the heavy curtains earlier and now hurried back to tell her friends they were almost ready to begin. Her heavy black costume prevented her from running too quickly, and her path was obstructed by the odd toad or fairy practising their lines.

Nearly everyone had been in the make-up department (Miss Dobson's own private office just off-stage, where Miss Dobson and some fifth formers were let loose with garish stage make-up, the results of which were a sight to behold).

Melissa reached her two friends. All three were nervous, and had only managed to have one quick run-through of the revised lines of the play, meeting straight after school that day and reciting as they walked home through the park.

She smiled encouragingly at the other two and took hold of their hands. "We'll be just fine," she said reassuringly. "We can do this, you'll see."

The sound of music from the hall stopped her from saying any more. Miss Dobson had liased with Mr Rankin, the music teacher, and he had put together a tape of somewhat spooky music to lend a bit more atmosphere to the play. The opening strains filled the hall, then died away to allow the Headmaster to speak.

Mr Perrie, the Head, welcomed everyone to the hall and, as promised, kept his speech as short as possible. The play was introduced and, before they knew it, the curtains were back and the girls were on stage!

"This one's for you, Geraldine," whispered Melissa as she took up her position.

Chapter Thirteen

The play opened with the scene where the three witches chopped off Jonathan's finger. There wasn't a sound to be heard in the assembly hall and Miss Dobson noted, with some satisfaction, that the audience seemed to hang on every word. There were audible gasps when the boy's finger was severed, and lots of loud boos and hisses as the witches performed their evil tricks. The curtains had been drawn over the windows which ran from ceiling to floor on one side of the hall so that, apart from the stage lights, there was almost complete darkness. The spooky music provided by Mr Rankin had been a burst of inspiration, Miss Dobson congratulated herself. The atmosphere in the hall was electric. She turned her attention back to the stage where the "raising of the dead," scene was being performed. She listened as Jenny repeated her lines:

"He grows warm. Let us complete our task."

Then, as the witches clasped the palms of their hands together, they began to recite the incantation:-

"From cold and dark you once did rise
More time on earth, that was your prize
But no more evil, no black spells pray
from us go, back into Hell."

Miss Dobson looked quizzically at the three girls then searched underneath her chair for her copy of the script. Though parts of what they had said seemed familiar, there was something about that little recitation that didn't seem quite right. She thumbed through her dog-eared copy, causing the parents behind her to tut at the rustle of paper, and quickly found the part she was looking for.

"But no more evil," – that was what they had said, wasn't it. And they should have said "To spread more evil, cash black spells." She glanced quickly at the faces of the audience nearest to her. No-one had noticed. And of course they wouldn't, she reassured herself, not unless they were familiar with the script, like she was. Just when she had thought everything was going to be all right, she thought wryly. When she had been so pleased to see Melissa, Jo and Jenny turn up for school today and assure her they had fully recovered and wouldn't let her down this evening. And they were getting their lines wrong!

A ripple of laughter stole through the audience at the antics of one of the trolls who had come on stage. Miss Dobson relaxed. It really didn't matter that one of the incantations had got a bit mixed up – she would put the script back under her chair and simply enjoy the rest of the evening. Funny thing was though, how all three of the girls had managed to get it wrong.

Jenny's mum seemed to be the first person to notice the change in temperature. As is usual at functions of this size, halls filled to capacity with people wearing winter coats, hats and boots tended to get a bit warm. Not so tonight. For Jenny's mother soon found that she was shivering from the cold and reaching for the coat she had discarded earlier to wrap around her shoulders. One by one, most of the people in the audience did the same thing, donning scarves and even gloves as Mr Perrie got up and walked over to check whether or not the heating was switched on. The radiator was ice cold. He whispered to Mr Rankin where he was going and left the Hall to go and speak to the janitor. Even the pupils on stage began to be aware of the icy cold in the Hall. Melissa and her two friends exchanged glances.

"I think it's working," whispered Melissa as she stamped her feet in a vain attempt to get warm. "The spirits are showing their displeasure – we have to keep it up."

Mr Perrie returned to the hall. He had been unable to find the janitor and he himself had no knowledge of the complexities of the heating system. As the door closed behind him, a blanket of warm air followed him into the room. He touched the radiator as he passed and was amazed to find that it was now warm. Mr Rankin smiled and gave him the thumbs up sign and he smiled back. He hadn't actually done anything to solve the problem of the cold, but Mr Rankin didn't need to know that, did he?

"It's Geraldine," Melissa thought to herself as the warm air reached her. "She's fighting back." She smiled and crossed her fingers as she continued with the play.

Acts 2 and 3 passed more or less uneventfully, though Miss Dobson did notice the girls get the occasional bit wrong. Nothing major, and nothing anyone else would pick up on, but maybe the last line of a spell would be incorrect, or a whole chant would be recited in reverse order. It really was strange. After all, it was only meant to be Jenny who had suffered the concussion.

The next act, the fourth and final one, started off well enough. It was the one which showed the witches conjure up all the powers of Satan and Hell in order to help them banish good from the earth. The three girls knew this was the important one, the one they just could not afford to get wrong . . . or right to be more accurate.

When the curtains opened, the huge, steaming cauldron had been placed centre stage and the three witches stood beside it. The trolls and hobgoblins, their helpers, danced around the stage, alternately grimacing and shouting at the audience.

The witches stood behind the cauldron and stared out at the sea of expectant faces. The spell book had been placed on a podium to the right and the eldest witch took her place beside it and began to read.

"In order for this spell to manifest itself properly," she began in a croaky voice, "it is important that only the freshest ingredients are used." She began to read out the list.

"1. The forked tongue of a living serpent .

"2. The fluffy tail of a white rabbit, which has been dipped in the still-warm blood of a first former."

All the first formers slunk lower into their seats. Miss Dobson scrabbled for her script but, as she did so, the doors of the hall started to bang open and shut, loudly, open and shut, open and shut, so that the icy blasts of air blew her script out of her grasp. The girls on stage had to raise their voices so they could be heard over the banging of the doors.

"3." called Melissa loudly, this time aided by Jo and Jenny.

"The brain of a Headmaster, to be boiled in the cauldron before being removed and eaten, slowly."

This was utter gobbledegook, thought Miss Dobson, rising to her feet. She was forced back into her seat, though, when all the windows blew wide open and flocks of crows flew into the assembly hall, squawking loudly, flying over the heads of the audience and adding to the general mayhem.

Mr Perrie was unexpectedly enjoying himself. These performances usually turned out to be tedious affairs and, on more than one occasion in the past, he had found himself nodding off to sleep. But not tonight. The acting and props had been excellent and the special effects! Well, they were quite something else! He must speak to Miss Dobson later about how she managed to get the crows to fly in the windows. That really was clever.

Melissa, Jo and Jenny were shouting now.

"4. 2 huge rats, one black and one brown, and a box full of squirming white maggots."

There was a screech on stage and Miss Dobson looked up to see that a fourth witch had joined the girls on stage. Who on earth was she? She peered at the witch's face but failed to recognise her.

"No!" the fourth witch screamed, outraged. "That's not what you're supposed to say, they're not the lines that were written for you. The lines you're meant to be reading are:-

"1. Cabbage and caterpillars, with compressed spiders' webs

"2. Bats blood mixed with deadly nightshade

"3. Foxglove juice and boars' grease

"And, lastly," she screeched, as her two sisters joined her on stage

"4. The pure white heart of a pretty young girl."

The audience were entranced. There were six witches on stage now, crows flying all around the Hall and the doors still banged open and shut. They couldn't wait to see what would happen next.

The smallest child on stage, Mary-Mary (given the unfortunate nickname by her friends because of her somewhat contrary nature), had tried to leave with the rest of the Trolls when the three older witches appeared, but she had been too slow. The witch nearest her grabbed her and tucked her under her arm, making her way towards the cauldron at the centre of the stage. The child screamed loudly.

"Let her be," called Melissa. "Your time on earth is over, go back to where you belong."

The witch laughed in response. "It's not over yet, my dear – look – we have the child, a child who possesses a pure, white heart, we merely need to find the rest of the ingredients and our reign here will continue for as long as we want it to."

But she grew weak, and knew her steps faltered as she toiled with the weight of the little girl. She knelt on the floor.

"Quickly, sister," she said, "help me,

help us, before we lose any more strength. You must open the child and remove her heart so that we may place it in the cauldron."

The witch pushed back the sleeve of her cloak, revealing the sharp knife-like objects which served as her fingers.

Suddenly, a light flickered on in the hall and some words were projected onto a screen. Leading the way, Melissa, Jo and Jenny began to chant the words, and were soon joined by the audience.

"Everything that's rotting here, we tell you now to go.

Go and join the evil one, in his dark place below.

Take your cauldrons and your tricks, rats and toads and spells

Go from us where you belong, we send you back to Hell."

The chant grew louder and louder as the audience repeated it over and over again. The three witches were now so weakened they could only lie on the stage and beg for mercy.

Jenny ran across the stage and grabbed hold of Mary-Mary, holding her tightly and making comforting noises that everything would be all right as the child cried.

Just before the final curtain closed Mr Perrie thought, though it could have been a trick of the light, that he saw the three figures disintegrate into three tiny piles of sand.

Chapter Fourteen

It was a bright morning which, though chilly, reminded the girls of the promise of summer days to come.

They placed the flowers they had brought with them at the foot of Geraldine Somers' grave. The wind and rain from the previous week had destroyed the flowers which had been there the last time the girls had visited the grave.

The three of them knelt and Melissa brushed some stray wet petals from the lettering on Geraldine's grave.

"She's at peace now, hopefully, and the actions we have taken should mean that her rest is never disturbed again," said

Melissa.

The girls had, in conjunction with Miss Dobson, destroyed every copy they could find of the stage play so that it would never be performed again. Though they hadn't disclosed every detail of the events which had taken place, Miss Dobson had been sufficiently spooked to agree with them that it would be best if the play were destroyed and never performed again.

"So?" began Jo as the girls stood up and made to leave. "Are you meeting Jonathan tonight? Not that I'm envious, you understand?" she smiled at Melissa.

Melissa and Jonathan getting together had been one of the few good things to come out of the staging of the play.

"Yes, I'm going to watch him play basketball and then we'll go for something to eat," Melissa smiled happily. "What about you two?"

Jo said she was going back for a second shot at ice skating with her niece.

"Got to get to grips with this sport," she laughed. "After all, the scar on my knee's almost gone from the last time."

Both girls looked towards Jenny, who smiled shyly. "I'm going to the hospital," she said, "to visit Danny."

Both her friends looked shocked.

"Danny Cottrill?"

"Yes, I know, the school bully, but I've been getting to know him over the past week or so since he came out of his coma and he's actually really nice. I didn't know his parents only moved here before he started high school and he was so insecure he acted the way he did to get some attention. Unwarranted attention, I might add. Anyway, the doctors say he's going to be all right, no permanent damage, and he should be out of hospital in a few more weeks."

The three girls walked down the path and out of the cemetery, closing the gate behind them.

"So, there's a happy ending after all," said Melissa as they walked off, heading for home.

What the girls didn't see were the pages which fluttered one by one onto Geraldine Somers' grave. The fresh flowers they had laid were almost obscured from view by the yellowed pages which fell on top of them. The top page fell, and any onlookers who passed would have been able to read the words *Oh Spirits Obey Us*, - Author, Geraldine Somers.